Chasing the Donkey

PROLOGUE

The ringing in his ears left him somewhat in a daze. They had been fighting for what seemed like forever. His hands felt slightly numb from firing his AK-47 for such a long time. He looked down at his feet and saw that maneuvering through all the rubble of the city, the sharp pieces of concrete left over from destroyed buildings had taken a heavy toll on his boots. He wasn't tired, just numb. He looked into the faces of the men in the circle. One by one. Some were pleading, some were praying, others were just staring blankly at the ground. They were Kurdish soldiers, not worth it to make a big show of. There were no cameras to record what was to come, he knew this would be over quickly. He saw ISIS fighters with knives in their hands approach the soldiers kneeling on the ground. Each fighter positioned himself behind one of the captives. They were all facing each other. The ringing in his ears seemed to drown out the noises around him in anticipation of what would come next. He had seen it before on the internet and the news. The widely publicized beheading and execution spectacles of the Islamic State did not leave much to the fantasy. Yet, even after seeing those videos so many times, this moment seemed surreal. The leader of the group said a few quick words, finished by "Allah Akbar." These were the starting words for the short but cruel event. One by one, each fighter pulled back the hair of the bound soldier at their feet and started slicing their throats, sawing away to sever the head completely. With the ringing in his ears seemingly more intense, he could not hear the noises the man in front of him made as he kept plunging his own knife into the soldier's neck. It took everyone between two to four minutes to finish the task. By the end, they all just tossed the severed heads in the middle of the circle of bleeding carcasses. Congratulating each other and yelling "Allah Akbar" over and over they walked towards their waiting trucks. Briefly, over the daze of what had just occurred, he thought of his mother and brother back in Germany. What would they say, if they knew what their little Daniel, now known as Abu Ahmed, had just done? With all the cheering that thought fleeted away quickly. He got in the bed of one of the white Toyota pick-up trucks and their little convoy sped back to their field headquarters.

CHAPTER 1

His footsteps echoed through the dark walls as he ran towards the light at the end of the tunnel. He heard the rumble and knew he would have to hurry up. With his 180 cm and strong build, Bastian had always been a fast runner. He picked up his pace and went into a dead sprint. Despite the weight of his heavy bag, his steps were light and effortless. He prayed the years of running cross country would pay off now. When he reached the top of the stairs, he heard that all too familiar voice and the rumbling started again. He knew it was almost too late, but he had to keep trying. While leaping down the stairs, taking several steps at a time, the rumbling shook the stairs and a strong wind pushed towards him. The subway-train had left the platform.

"Fuck!" He yelled.

An elderly woman whom he had startled when he ran past her eyed him with a frown while shaking her head disapprovingly.

"Sorry," he mumbled, as she walked past him towards the center of the platform.

Not being on time annoyed him. He had already left the university library late because of an engaging discussion about the legal and ethical issues of monitoring extremists by the Bundesnachrichtendienst, Germany's intelligence service, and the Gemeinsames Terrorabwehrzentrum (GTAZ) with his law study group. With the growing influence of Islamic extremist groups in Europe, surveillance and measures to prevent events like the terror attacks in London and Madrid became almost everyday topics. Bastian was in his last year of law school and constitutional law was going to be his future field of work. He had always had a knack for debate about personal rights vs government surveillance, but his left leaning views on that topic had changed when he entered the military service. He had spent time in Germany's elite military unit Kommando Spezialkräfte and his deployments to places like Iraq and Afghanistan had shown him the complexity of war and conflict. He learned quickly that nothing is how it seems. There was always more to a situation than visible on first sight. In spite of what many of his peers thought, he realized that not every local Afghan farmer was an extremist or supporter of the Taliban. The bigger picture is a mosaic of a multitude of pieces. The reasons for the farmer Ahmed to bury an improvised explosive device (IED) in the road revolved oftentimes around protecting his family, rather than an ideology filled hate against the strange tall soldiers from a country halfway around the world. His understanding that you need all the information to judge a situation properly served him well during his studies after leaving the military. This and his tireless work ethic,had earned him an intern position with the Bundesverfassungsschutz, Germany's domestic security service. It was tasked with intelligence-gathering on threats concerning the democratic order, the existence and security of the federation or one of its states, and the peaceful coexistence of peoples. Bastian was excited to begin his position in the legal office in a few months after he graduated. None of this mattered right now though, because he knew she would be disappointed. How could he have lost track of time on his mother's birthday? She was probably sitting alone in her apartment waiting for her sons. They hardly heard from his brother these days. He would call once in a while to reassure his mother that he was doing ok in the refugee camp where he volunteered in Turkey. But Bastian could always tell by his brother's voice when he was lying. He was just hoping his mother couldn't. Bastian doubted Daniel would magically appear for the birthday, which meant his mother would already be in a bad mood. He glanced at the digital information sign hanging from the platform ceiling. Ten more minutes until the next train would arrive.

When the bright yellow train finally arrived, Bastian practically got the whole car to himself. The rush had passed and the commuters had most likely gotten home from work by now. Instead of having to stand between sweaty and stressed strangers, he got a row of seats to himself by the window, towards the back of the cart. One of the benefits of being late, he thought. The only other passengers in the cart were a gray haired man and two teenagers. The man looked half asleep, wearing a dirty, dark trench coat, a scarf and knitted mittens, even though it was late April. The teenagers, sitting together at the front, were caught up in a mix of awkwardly making out, and giggling while taking pictures with their phones of the nearly-passed out man. Bastian considered saying something, as he assumed the old man didn't want his picture taken, but decided not to when they started making out again. Instead, he focused his attention to the small TV screen hanging from the ceiling and tried to block out the publicly affectionate teenagers. The news headline on the screen said something about a group of Syrian soldiers having been beheaded by ISIS militants.

When the train arrived at Ullsteinstrasse, Bastian got off. There was a light drizzle outside, and it had started to get dark. For a second he was blinded by the headlights from a car passing by. He had to take the bus from here. As he walked towards the bus stop he noticed the flower shop across the street. Luckily there was not much traffic, so he crossed the street on a red man. He bought the first big bouquet of pink roses he saw by the counter, and ran back across the street just in time to catch the bus.

Fifteen minutes later, he was standing outside his mother's apartment building in Steglitz. It was a large, white four story building from the 1950s, surrounded by similar apartment buildings. Each apartment had a balcony with a red fence; some of them had flower beds hanging from them. The street was dark now, only lit up by the occasional streetlight, but Bastian could see that the tall trees on both sides of the road had started to grow green leaves. It was a nice neighborhood to grow up in. There were plenty of kids to play with, and a playground right around the corner. Bastian walked up to the front door, barely avoiding stepping in a puddle. The doorbell screamed "beeep", as he pushed the little button next to his last name; "Heidrich". The door buzzed open, and Bastian entered the small entrance hall. The brick walls were cold and white, and his footsteps made loud echoing thumps as he walked up the wooden stairs to the second floor. She must have heard him coming, because his mother opened the door before he had the chance to knock. She smiled at him, but still had that all too familiar ever-present look of concern on her face. Her naturally light blonde hair was pulled up in a loose knot, and her blue eyes lit up when she saw him. Bastian greeted his mother with a long hug and the words "Happy Birthday," and handed her the big bouquet of pink roses.

She accepted them and asked "Where have you been Sebastian? You said you'd be here two hours ago."

His mother was one of the few people that called him by his full name. It was his younger brother who had started to call him Bastian, but by now it seemed almost everyone did.

"I know, I'm so sorry, mum, I was stuck in a study group, but I'm here now!"

"Well, come on in," she commanded.

While she closed the door, he hung up his jacket on one of the hooks on the wall and then followed her through the narrow hallway, to the dining table in the living room where she placed the pink flowers in a glass vase she had grabbed from one of the cupboards. The apartment wasn't big, but it was enough for his mother. It even had a small guest room which had been Daniel's until he was old enough to move out.

Their father had passed on their mom's birthday when Bastian was only 8 years old. He only faintly remembered him, but he was all too aware of the hole in their lives his death had caused. His mom's day of celebration had become a mix between grief and awkwardness. She was never sure whether it was ok for her to move on and find another partner. After all these years, she still loved him. Her sons were her only living connection to her late husband, since both of her and his parents had passed early in their lives as well. Actually, that was the common ground on which their mutual friend Gabriella had introduced them. She always found it morbid of her friend to make that the ice breaker, but it had worked. The few years she had with Bjorn, her sons' father, were probably the happiest of her life. He was the epitome of what a man should be like to her. Strong, tall, smart and an amazing father. The cancer took all that away within only 6 months. Now, Sebastian and Daniel were her only living memory of him. Their childhood home before their father's death was in a similar apartment building in the same neighborhood. That apartment had been bigger, but too expensive for their mother alone to keep. It wasn't so much that she couldn't afford it. The money they had saved and Bjorn's life insurance money ensured that there would not be any money issues. Her main complaint was that it was simply too big for her alone, and it took too long to clean all the rooms, but Bastian suspected she was just saying that so they would be happy for her, and not sad when she sold the old apartment. The new one had a small entrance hall with two doors to the right leading to the guest room and his mother's room, and two doors to the left leading to a small storage and the bathroom. The narrow hallway led to the living- and dining room. There was a large window on the end wall and a glass door leading to a small balcony. In the left corner was a small kitchen. The walls in the kitchen corner had a warm, light blue color, matching the flowery, turquoise couch in the living room, placed in front of the big window. The rest of the walls were plain white, but the room felt warm because of all the candles, pillows, furry blankets and other decorations his mother had stuffed the room with. He had once expressed that it was a little over the top, to which his mother had replied that it is a decorative style called shabby chique or something strange like that. She gestured him to sit by the dining table while placing a pot of coffee next to the cake that was already waiting.

After he had poured himself some coffee, he asked her about Daniel. While he talked, he helped himself to a large piece of cheesecake his mom had made. He knew it wasn't her favorite, but Bastian and his brother couldn't get enough of it. She loved her sons and did what she could to give them a reason to visit. Bastian always smiled to himself when he thought about it. She didn't have to bribe him with cake to come over, he loved spending time with the family. But he also didn't mind it.

"So, uhm, did Daniel call today?" He asked, stuffing his mouth full of cheesecake while trying not to be too unappetizing in front of his mother.

"Yes, we video chatted earlier today. Did he tell you, his beard is fully grown out again now?"

She didn't wait for an answer. She knew the brothers hadn't spoken in a while. Bastian had known Daniel was keeping something from him, and when he pushed him on it a few weeks ago they had a falling out.

"I haven't said anything to you about this, Sebastian, but I have suspected for a while that Daniel has been keeping something from us."

She was leaning forward with her palms folded on the table, staring at Sebastian with a serious expression. So his mum could tell when Daniel was lying.

"I didn't confront him about it earlier because I was worried he would stop calling." Like he stopped calling me, Bastian thought. "But I asked him about it today, Sebastian," she continued. "I asked him to be honest with me as my birthday present. And I was right. Daniel is not in some refugee camp in Turkey anymore. I even doubt he ever was. He is in Syria with some militia group that's fighting against the regime there."

Bastian dropped the fork as he swallowed the big piece of cake in his mouth, and stared at his mum, not sure if he had understood what she was saying.

"He was talking about how he's not only helping the Arabic people, but that it is what Allah wants from him, and.." She stopped for a second. Holding back her tears, Bastian thought. "And... You know how he is." She stammered. "He assured me he is OK, and he says he is getting his own apartment, and..."

"Wait!" Bastian interrupted. All of a sudden he noticed new lines on her face and how small she looked sitting by the end of the oval dining table.

"So are you saying he's joined ISIS or something?" he said in disbelief.

She mumbled; "Sebastian, I don't know."

CHAPTER 2

Bastian splashed the cold water on his face and turned off the faucet. Then reached for the towel and padded his face dry. He stared at his reflection in the bathroom mirror. His blue eyes, bushy eyebrows and dark blonde hair were the same as his brother's. Even though Sebastian was five years older than Daniel, he had been told many times how much they looked alike. Except he currently was clean shaven with a short, side parted haircut, and Daniel had short hair and a big, messy beard the last time he saw him. Not the styled hipster kind of beard, but a bushy, almost funny-looking kind, that had made Bastian laugh when he first saw it. Daniel had been insulted of course, and Bastian had apologized to avoid an argument. It had been almost three months since he'd last seen Daniel now. His mother had told him that when his brother had come to say goodbye before he left, around that same time, he had shaved off his beard. He looked like his old self again, their mother had said.

It had been surreal when Daniel had first converted to Islam. Bastian, himself not overly into religion, had never understood what Daniel found in Islam. He was pretty sure they had had a happy childhood, given the circumstances of their father's early death. Perhaps his death affected Daniel more than Bastian, since he couldn't recall their father at all. Only the omnipresence of this stranger in all the pictures with his mom. Daniel had aspired to be like his brother throughout their childhood. Until high school that was. He became one of the punk kids while Bastian had been one of the jocks who loved soccer. This was when Daniel started acting out, and his grades were dropping from good to barely passing. When his mom took him to a doctor, he was diagnosed with ADHD. Bastian always had a feeling that this put a label on his brother, which he could never quite get rid of. In fact, it had seemed to make things even worse and Daniel barely got through school. Bastian had tried to help him as much as he could, but Daniel didn't want his help. He had always been stubborn, and wanted to do things himself. The diagnosis had opened a rift between them, and it had seemed to only worsen when Bastian informed Daniel and their mother about his plans to go to the Bundeswehr, Germany's army, after graduating from high school. It was soon after that Bastian had caught his younger brother smoking weed on the playground around the corner. He suspected Daniel had tried harder drugs as well over the years. Being away from home a lot for training and deployments, he had to rely on what he witnessed when on leave at home or whatever little bit of information he could pry from his brother whenever they talked.

About three years ago, Bastian had learned from his mother about his brother's newfound faith in Islam. At first, it seemed like a good thing. He appeared really happy, and seemingly got his act together. As if he had a new purpose in life. He got a job at a gym that he kept for a long time, and he had stopped partying and doing drugs. While Bastian welcomed his brother's abstinence from drugs, other changes seemed odd to him. Daniel had always loved a good party and rock music, and had even played some guitar in high school, so it was quite a change when he claimed music was a sin and completely stopped listening to it. Religion had never been something Bastian was interested in from the standpoint of believing in a higher being. He enjoyed the rhetoric and discussion about scripture. He had even tried to engage Daniel in discussion about the Koran and why music was a sin, to which he had replied by quoting from Soorat Luqmaan: "And of mankind is he who purchases idle talks (i.e. music, singing) to mislead (men) from the path of Allah…" He had even expressed his concerns on a few occasions that their mother would go to hell because she didn't cover her hair. Discussions like this quickly developed into small arguments, driving the brothers even further apart.

Daniel's sense of style had changed too. Bastian had seen pictures on Facebook of Daniel wearing a conservative Arabic robe and hat, while handing out flyers advocating Islam in Berlin. The style was a drastic change from the angry teenager who wore black hoodies and pierced his eyebrow. Bastian knew Daniel had visited a mosque with a bad reputation a few times, and now he found himself regretting not confronting him about it. Although, he wasn't quite sure, if that even could have made a difference. While the angry teenager might have been gone, it was now replaced by something else. Something more assertive and demanding. Since Daniel had started attending the new mosque, he had become increasingly vocal about sin and how to walk in the path of the prophet Mohammed (peace be upon him, Daniel would say) and abiding by Allah's will. This coincided with comments on how Israel, the USA and Europe were to blame for about everything going wrong in the Middle East. One of his remarks: "There will never be peace in the Levant and the Arabic world until Israel and its puppet master, the United States, are wiped of the face of the earth!" now rushed back into Bastian's mind. How could he have been so blind the entire time? His brother had become exactly what he had been fighting against on the various battlefields during his deployments to Afghanistan and Africa. The question of how and why remained. Bastian broke his stare at the reflection in the mirror and put the hand towel he had used for his face back on the hanger.

He closed the bathroom door and walked to the living room where he stopped in the door. His mother was sitting on the light-green, three-seat couch by the window. She had put away what was left of the cake and had turned on a crime show on TV. Sebastian leaned against the doorframe and folded his arms.

"Why are you so calm?" He asked with a somewhat critical tone. Her gaze moved from the TV over to him. "Why are you taking this so lightly?"

"Oh, Sebastian, I'm not taking this lightly. But I told you, I've been suspecting this for a while and I am not sure what I could do at this point."

She reached for the remote and lowered the volume on the TV.

"I know this must be a shock to you, you always see the best in your brother. But you didn't see him as often as I did, and you don't talk to him that often anymore, so there was no way you could have known."

He didn't know what to say. He should have known, he thought. How could he not have seen it?

"Come watch TV with me?" She asked and patted the couch next to where she was sitting, gesturing him to join her.

He thought for a moment, then looked at his watch.

"I should go," he said. He didn't want his mother to know how much this bothered him, but she probably already knew. "If I go now I'll catch the next bus."

She looked a bit disappointed, but said; "Ok, honey. Give me a call when you get home." He gave her a hug goodbye, and left.

CHAPTER 3

He didn't call his mother that night. It was almost midnight by the time he was finally back at his studio apartment in Schöneberg. He had told her he would catch the bus home, but he was too upset to head straight home. He needed to clear his head. He had wandered around Steglitz for a while before walking home. He kept zigzagging on a very indirect path to his place. Out of habit, he had locked himself in immediately after gently pushing the door shut behind him. He kicked off his shoes while he fumbled for the light switch on the wall. An old lamp, hanging from a cord from the ceiling, lit up the apartment. The apartment was quite small, and he could probably afford a bigger one with the combination of his student loans and his military education benefits. But Bastian liked his apartment. He liked the fact that it was directly under the roof of the building and he didn't need more space. The low rent had allowed him to save up some money, without even having a job in addition to his studies. The room he was standing in contained both a living room and kitchen. The ceiling was high, and there were two large windows on the outer wall. A tall but small dining table and two barstools separated the kitchen next to the entrance door from the living room space. The living room area consisted of a bookshelf, desk, TV and a gray couch decorated with three patterned pillows his mother had bought for him. Apparently she thought his simplistic style, or lack of style as she had said, was depressing which is why she had bought pillows, curtains and a furry carpet for his apartment. In his bedroom, the only furniture was a bed and another bookshelf. Both of his bookshelves were packed with books he had bought on different occasions, most of which he still had not read. He liked the idea of reading, but didn't have the time, and sometimes not the patience to actually do so as often as he'd like. Bastian took his laptop out from his backpack, and tossed the pack on the floor. Right now he didn't care about his books, even though he had spent a small fortune on them at the beginning of the school year. He moved the mess from his desk between the windows, a few notebooks and sheets of paper and opened his MacBook. He wanted to call his brother, but didn't have his phone number. It was always Daniel who called them. He had a new phone now, and when Bastian had called his old number, the phone was either off or without service.

He opened Facebook and examined his brother's profile. There wasn't much info on it. A few pictures with Arabic writing that probably quoted the Quran, and a few with a political message about the suffering of the Syrian people under the Assad regime. Daniel had deleted all pictures of himself and other information a long time ago, but Bastian was hoping to find at least a hint as to where he was and what the hell he was thinking. "Where are you?" he typed in the chat. But he knew that sometimes it could take days before Daniel replied. Plus, they weren't exactly on the best terms after Bastian had called him out about lying about his situation in Turkey (which he had been right about, by the way), so he might even take longer than that this time. But Bastian couldn't wait for days. He wanted to look through his friend list to see who and where they were, but that part of the profile was private. Bastian felt the frustration growing stronger. There was literally no useful information on the profile. He closed the laptop, leaned back in the chair and rubbed the back of his neck while thinking. He didn't know any of Daniel's Muslim friends, but he did know the Mosque he had been frequently going to before he had left. The Fussilet mosque in Moabit had a bad reputation of inviting radical imams to speak and had even been mentioned in the news on a few occasions. He had to go there. Maybe someone there knew where Daniel was, he thought. But he didn't want to simply walk over there alone and unprepared. He didn't know if they would even let him into the mosque, let alone talk to him.

He had learned some Arabic while in the military, as well as the basics about Islam and local customs and courtesies. It was great knowledge for the battlefield, but probably wouldn't get him very far now. He thought for a brief moment and then made the decision to ask his friend Adnan from law school for help. He had been skeptical of Adnan when they initially met on their first day of school, but back then he had been skeptical about everyone and everything, a habit that had formed during his deployments and which had taken him a while to move past. Adnan was the son of Iraqi immigrants. Adnan's father Sayed had been part of the Baath Party under Saddam Hussein's rule. He was never fully supportive of the dictator, but he had a family and needed to take care of his wife and kids. Being a party member had opened many doors that would have been closed otherwise. After the U.S. invasion of

Iraq in 2003, Adnan's family fled the country and settled in their new home in Germany. Sayed was lucky and quickly found work as a professor of Islamic history and politics at the Freie Universität in Berlin. He valued hard work and had an appreciation for history in order to understand current events. Things he shared with Bastian and one of the reasons Sayed liked Adnan to be friends with him, despite his son being 5 years younger than his friend. Bastian took his phone and sent an SMS to his friend.

"Need your help. Can we meet tomorrow for lunch? It's important!"

He received a response a few moments later.

"Sure, let's meet at the caf on campus at 12."

"Great," he thought.

Hopefully Adnan would be able to help him get into the mosque and find out if someone there knew where Daniel was, or even better, could get in touch with him. He didn't want to assume that every person attending that mosque was an ISIS supporter, but Daniel had been attending there too, and apparently he was. Someone there had to know him. And whether there was an actual recruiter involved, or if it had just been Daniel and some friends who came up with the idea and went through with it, either way, he was certain the mosque would be the best place to start. He opened his laptop again and glanced at the clock in the upper right hand corner of the screen. It was almost one in the morning, but Bastian didn't think he'd be able to sleep yet, even though he had classes in the morning. He opened Safari and googled "ISIS". Lots of pictures of black flags with white writings, as well as men wearing black clothes and covering their faces popped up on the screen. He scrolled through them. They were always carrying guns or large daggers and were often in formation, as if they were in some kind of parade. Sometimes there were people wearing orange jumpsuits in the pictures as well. These would be the victims of beheading or some other horrible way of dying that would bring more attention to the terrorist group. Bastian wondered if Daniel's face was hidden behind one of the black masks in one of these pictures. He couldn't believe Daniel was capable of something like this. Had Daniel turned into someone able and willing to behead people? His brother had been rebellious, but Bastian couldn't even imagine his brother doing any of those things. If he in fact had joined ISIS there had to be more to it than what Bastian could see. Although he couldn't think of even one excuse for killing innocent people like that. He scrolled through some more pictures. In some of them there was a parade of pickup trucks with men waving flags and guns. It looked very staged and reminded him of pirates on a ship from a movie, except the ship was pickup trucks. The images were of good quality, not something that could have been done with a phone.

"Who took all these pictures?" he wondered.

Probably not ordinary people unfortunate to be living in those areas, and certainly not the mainstream media. This meant they had to have their own skilled and extremely productive media (or rather propaganda) team. He googled "ISIS media," and found several news articles discussing their media use. Unfortunately most of the videos being discussed had been deleted, but he discovered the name of ISIS' own, fairly professional "Al Hayat." He then found several recruitment videos, which talked about the glory of fighting for Allah, showed battle scenes and featured some Arabic singing throughout.

CHAPTER 4

"Riing", the old fashioned ringtone on his phone woke him up. He had fallen asleep with his face on the computer keyboard sometime while watching ISIS propaganda videos. He stretched his arms and felt his back crack. He rubbed his face and could feel the imprints of the keyboard on his right cheek. "Riiing," the cell phone rang again, seeming extra aggressive. He picked it up and saw it was Adnan.

"Hey, where are you, man, I'm at the cafeteria waiting for you," Adnan's voice inquired through the phone.

Bastian looked at the clock on his phone. It showed 12.15.

"Shit, I've overslept!" He stood up so fast his chair fell on the floor with a loud bang. "Ah, I'm so sorry, can we meet later today instead?" he asked, still not quite awake.

"Sure. Just come over to my house around 5pm. My parents will love seeing you."

Bastian arrived at Adnan's place 10 minutes early. It always gave him a sense of security to be overly punctual. Despite having been here numerous times, he still checked the surroundings. He wasn't sure whether that was something he had always done or something the military had instilled in him. The apartment Adnan's family owned was located in the neighborhood called Zehlendorf, in walking distance between the Freie Universität and the mosque in Zehlendorf. Adnan's father Sayed took advantage of that fact and walked to work most of the time. He had once told Bastian that these walks to and from work were his "me time", when he could reflect on things that were on his mind. The family owned an apartment at the corner of Hubertusbader Strasse and Knausstrasse, an intersection typical for this part of the city. Quiet, with small buildings and plenty of foliage that provided privacy. Bastian had always thought it felt serene, almost out of place compared to his own neighborhood. He could see why Adnan's father had chosen this place for his family's new home after they had escaped the chaos and the violence of Iraq. Bastian's thoughts started to drift.

He remembered his childhood, the love of his mother, the brotherly bantering with his younger brother, the struggles of their adolescent years, his time in the military, war, friends dying, coming home, adjusting to a life outside of the uniform, the news about Daniel. He could feel his heart starting to race. He heard voices and noises from his former fellow soldiers. Despite it being a normal summer evening with clear skies and a comfortable 20 degrees Celsius, he started sweating. He smelled it again. He knew it wasn't real. It didn't matter though. That smell had itself ingrained into him. The mix of iron, gun powder and burnt flesh. It was just a flash in front of his eyes, one of his fellow soldiers torn apart by an Improvised Explosive Device, Bastian trying to help, despite it being too late [. He tried to calm down. His breathing was fast, it felt like his heart was going to rip a hole into his chest. He steadied himself by leaning with his right hand against the iron fence that surrounded Adnan's apartment building. The cold of the metal against his callused palm seemed to help. Slowly he relaxed. The smells, sounds and pictures faded. This was one of the more severe panic attacks he had had in a while. They usually only happened when he was under a lot of stress. He could deal with the lack of sleeping and the bad dreams since the military, but he didn't like these panic attacks.

When he was sure he had calmed down and his breathing was normal again, he told himself "Get it together already" and walked through the gate to the front door of the building. He had to focus on what he was there for, to find his little brother. There were only 4 apartments in the building and as always he looked at the names for a moment. He had them memorized from day one, but every time he came over he looked at them to make sure they were still the same. He pushed the button next to Adnan's last name; Ayoub.

The doorbell rang, and a few seconds later, a young woman's voice asked "Yes?" through the intercom.

Bastian recognized the voice.

"Hey, Hafsa, it's Bastian," he replied to Adnan's younger sister.

"Bastian! Come on in!"

The door unlocked, and Bastian stepped into the circular entrance hall. The walls were high and had a warm, light yellow color. The tiled floor was white with a black striped pattern. Four mailboxes were hanging on the wall to the right, and there was a big dark wooden apartment door on the right wall, and one on the left. The circular stairs in the middle of the hall led down to the basement and up to the second floor where Adnan lived. Bastian started up the stairs. The steps were wide, but low, so Bastian took long strides, two steps at the time. They lead to a small, indoor balcony with a view down at the entrance door and the hall. Bastian took off his dark blue hooded jacket and wiped the small droplets of sweat from his forehead with the back of his hand before knocking on the big, dark wooden door to the right. Soon after, a small, bony, teenage girl with waist long black hair opened the door for him. "Hi Hafsa, how are you?" Bastian asked. "I'm good" she replied awkwardly and quickly looked down as she stepped to the side and gestured him to come in. Hafsa was seventeen, but Bastian thought she looked younger because of how small she was. Or maybe it was because of how shy she always seemed. "Bastian!" Adnan appeared from the living room door. Bastian gave Hafsa a friendly pat on the shoulder before he walked down the hall towards Adnan. The hall had a typical old Berlin style, with white walls, and high ceilings adorned with stucco. The only thing that could give away the family's Middle Eastern background was the long dark red Persian carpet decorating the floor. The living room was a bit more telling. It had the same architectural style with a high ceiling, detailed moldings and ceiling rose. However, instead of a traditional chandelier, an upside down pear shaped lamp with a pointy bottom was hanging from it. It was dark metal with a detailed pattern that allowed the light to shine through. Bookshelves and pictures covered the walls. Plants filled the room, especially around the big windows, and another big, dark red Persian carpet made the room seem smaller than it probably was. The coffee table by the dark brown couch was small and round with wooden legs and the top was a round metal tray with a similar detailed pattern as on the lamp. There was also a brown leather pouffe in the sitting area, and a big water pipe stored away in the corner next to the couch. Adnan sat down on the couch and lowered the volume on the Arabic show on the flat screen TV, hanging on the wall.

"Well, what's up?" he asked.

Bastian was used to giving reports from his time in the military and later during his law studies. He briefly described to his friend what he recently had learned about his brother after meeting with his mother. Adnan was quiet and just stared at Bastian for a moment. They all had heard about foreign fighters from all over Europe joining the Islamic State, but it wasn't every day one actually knew one of them personally.

"So, how can I help?" he asked.

Bastian hadn't figured out a full-scale plan yet. First of all, he needed more information.

"Can you get me into the Fussilet mosque? Maybe help me find one of the ISIS recruiters there?"

Adnan's reaction was unexpected. His face contorted right before he busted out in laughter.

"Are you kidding me?!" he eventually grinned. "That mosque has a reputation for a reason. Besides, do you really think they just let you waltz in there and ask questions about the people who sign up young guys for one of the currently most hated organizations, just because you have your Arabic buddy with you? It doesn't work that way. You are way to light skinned and blue eyed for that my friend. They'd probably kick us out right away, thinking we are snitches for the police."

"Well, do you have a better idea?" Bastian asked, in a tone that was a little more hostile then he intended to.

His thoughts were still racing and he didn't need his best friend's mockery at the moment.

"You need a crash course in how to act like a pious radical. A Daesh course if you will."

Bastian knew his friend was trying to lighten up the situation by finishing his idea with a joke, and also that he was right. Surely, an organization like that would not take everyone coming from the streets without some sort of vetting process.

"It's 17.30 now" Adnan said. "My parents should be home soon. Stay for dinner, and after, we will talk to them about giving you some pointers on how to act like a good extremist. Sounds good?"

"Alright" Bastian said.

"In the meantime, you can help me convince Hafsa to turn down her god awful Justin Bieber love song collection," Adnan said.

He grimaced and continued, "Seriously! Why can't these kids listen to something proper, like the Sex Pistols?"

Bastian had to smile.

About thirty minutes later Adnan's dad Sayed came through the door carrying a briefcase and several plastic bags from different restaurants in one hand, and five boxes of takeout food balancing on top of each other in the other. As he pushed the door shut behind him with his foot, the boxes swayed dangerously. Adnan must have noticed it too, because he hurried over to his father and took the boxes.

"Oh, hi Bastian, it has been way too long since your last visit, so I figured we should celebrate a little bit" he said when he noticed Bastian in the living room door.

The Justin Bieber music was finally turned off as Hafsa came out from her room to help with the food. Adnan hadn't exaggerated, "she really likes this god awful music," Bastian thought.

"Your mother had to work late again, but I got some extra dinner she can warm up later," he said as the family made their way into the kitchen.

Their mother Rana worked at the Berlin office of Amnesty International where she planned events, demonstrations and signature campaigns. Ever since the emergence of ISIS, she had become extremely busy. Bastian had noticed she often worked late, but from what he could tell when he met her, she seemed to love it. The three of them unpacked the food and set the table in just a couple of minutes, while Sayed freshened up in the bathroom. Before Bastian knew it, it looked like a home cooked meal had been served. Or more accurately, several meals. Sayed loved food, to him it was the key to the world's cultures. The smells of all the different dishes created an aroma that Bastian could not put into words. There was a big pile of Naan bread and several bowls with different content and colors. Some of it looked like sauces and some of it had meat in them. There was Mezah, a common food in many Arabic countries, but also spaghetti with meatballs, sauerkraut, Norwegian Rhubarb pudding, hummus, Irish corned beef and French chocolate mousse. Sayed Ayoub showed his love of life, his family and his kids through food. And judging by what Bastian saw on the dinner table, he had a lot of love. Before they started eating, Sayed prepared two large plates for his wife. He knew she had a weakness for the sauerkraut and the rhubarb pudding, which suited Adnan just fine. He always put on an overly exaggerated face of disgust when he smelled the kraut. In keeping with his opinion on this specific dish, he urged his father to just give his mother the entire bowl. Bastian's favorite was the chicken and the beef rib steak which were marinated in spicy sauces. It had a strong taste of garlic, and some of it was a bit spicier than what he was used to. He was glad there was a big can of water on the table because he emptied the first glass after only one bite of Nan bread dipped in one of the spicier sauces.

During the meal Adnan retold the story he had just heard from Bastian. When he finished, Bastian looked at Sayed's somber expression and said

"I just don't understand what he's thinking."

"Well, the situation in Iraq and Syria, with the civil war and the emergence of ISIL, or simply IS as they now call themselves, is a complex issue with a myriad of factors involved," the professor said, "I can try to give you a better understanding of it."

With that, Sayed sat back in his chair and put on a demeanour Bastian assumed was typical for when he taught at the university. Right when he opened his mouth to speak: "But we like to call them Daesh, not ISIS," Adnan jumped in before he could speak.

"That's right," Sayed agreed. "Calling them the Islamic State implies that we acknowledge them as an actual sovereign state, which we obviously don't. Daesh however, is an abbreviation of the Arabic way to say the Islamic state. It is a challenge to their legitimacy, dismissing their aspirations. to *acknowledge and address them as such*. They want to be acknowledged and addressed as exactly what they claim to be, using the pompously long and in my opinion delusional name the group created. Saying Daesh seems derogatory to them, since it is made and funny-sounding word."

He smiled with raised eyebrows behind his square glasses. Bastian didn't answer, but nodded his head in agreement.

"Anyways, I am drifting off topic. So, you've heard of the Arab spring, right?"

Sayed asked, but didn't wait for Bastian to answer.

"This was a wave of demonstrations and protests in the Arab world which started in Tunisia at the end of 2010. The demonstrators wanted more freedom and democracy. But when the spring reached Syria, Bashar al-Assad, the president, or dictator there responded by sending the Syrian army on the protesters, many of whom were students. This resulted in hundreds of civilian deaths. However, Assad wasn't able to stop the protesters. Instead the demonstrations escalated and the protestors armed themselves and several rebellious militia groups around the country emerged. One of these groups was Daesh. Unlike other militia groups, Daesh does not want more democracy and freedom. Instead they want to create an Islamic caliphate where their strict interpretation of sharia laws applies and where al-Baghdadi rules as the caliph. They want their state to cover the Levant, which basically is the area south of Turkey, including Syria and Iraq of course." The professor paused as if to make a point, and then added; "and even Israel." He then focused his attention on carefully cutting a piece of meat on his plate.

"I'm sorry, but this still doesn't explain how someone can leave their whole life behind to join a terrorist group," Bastian muttered.

Sayed nodded as he swallowed some sauerkraut and took a sip of his red wine while looking at him.

"No, of course not. When seen from the outside it is always difficult to understand how there can be any logical reasoning behind such evil. But the truth is your brother most likely thinks he is fighting a very noble cause. He thinks he is helping to free an oppressed people from a dictator. However, he also thinks he is being a good Muslim by doing this, and that he will be rewarded in Jannah, which is what we call paradise. You see, a good Muslim should always try to do as the prophet Muhammad did. That is why so many Muslim men have beards, because the prophet is said to have had a beard. The prophet also created an Islamic state, which is why some see it as their duty as Muslims to participate in the creation of a new Islamic state. Also, according to the Qur'an, those who die while fighting for Islam will achieve martyrdom and go to Jannah. This is what some call jihad. However there are many interpretations of what exactly jihad is. Typically it is said that there are two types of jihad; the inner struggle to be a good Muslim, and the outer struggle. It is this outer struggle that some call a holy war, but as I said there are many interpretations of this- some of which are very controversial, and most Muslims do not agree with these violent interpretations."

Sayed paused again and took another sip of his red wine before adding; "however, this way of interpreting jihad is fairly new and much of it can be accredited to the philosopher Sayed Qutb. It was his philosophy that all of these so-called mujahideen fighting their holy war rely on."

Bastian frowned and felt a bit confused.

"I thought that term referred to the Afghan resistance fighters back when the Soviet Union invaded Afghanistan?!" Bastian said.

"Mujahideen just means someone who is fighting an inner or outer ji-had" Adnan explained.

"Yes, the term is not necessarily related to extremism or terrorism, al-though Daesh use the word of their supporters." Sayed added.

"Now, Daesh traces its origin back to the 2003 U.S. invasion of Iraq," Adnan said. Immediately after the disposing of Saddam Hussein, the interim Iraq administration, gave the order to "de-Baathify" the country. Right, dad?"

"Yes," Sayed responded, "this affected civilian and military services, leaving hundreds of thousands of Sunnis, formerly loyal to Saddam Hussein's regime, without a job. Imagine it as over 300,000 potential insurgents being created overnight. Al Qaeda realized this potential and decided to capitalize on the anger created by the new government. Al Qaeda in Iraq was created to wage an insurgency against U.S. troops in Iraq. Simultaneously to resisting the foreign occupation, they also fought a sectarian war against Iran-backed Shiite militias in central Iraq."

"Wait a minute. Nobody foresaw that? Why would the U.S. do some-thing so foolish?" Bastian asked.

"Excellent question," Sayed said. Bastian could see how Adnan's father enjoyed this opportunity to discuss modern politics and history. "My best guess is that the head of that interim administration, Mr. Bremer, is a child of the Cold War, who didn't have much experience or expertise on the Middle East, which he made up for with plenty of ego. Instead of listening to experts and intelligence available, he decided to follow the model the United States had used on Germany after World War 2 to de-Nazify the country. At this point, I believe he simply wanted to leave his mark. A very sad legacy, if you ask me."

"I understand the anger and frustration of the Iraqi, but why turn to such extremism as practiced by ISIS?"

"Initially," Sayed answered, "Al Qaeda in Iraq focused on the U.S. occupation, but throughout the conflict, many of their members were imprisoned in U.S.-run prisons, such as "Camp Bucca". What at first seems counterintuitive actually played into their hands. Those places actually turned into meeting halls where they were able to meet up and radicalize. Guarded by young American soldiers without knowledge of the culture or even the basics of the Arabic language, the inmates were able to freely share information and communicate. Scary, right?"

Bastian shook his head in disbelief over what he was hearing.

"How did nobody see that?"

"To be fair," Sayed said, "don't underestimate the chaos of war. You have been to conflicts yourself, but Iraq was more in turmoil than Afghanistan. Quite possibly even more convoluted because of all the different players involved seeking to revenge their family, tribe or simply try to seize a fragile situation to pursue whatever goal they might have. Anyways, despite all of that, by 2007 the U.S.-installed, Shiite government in Baghdad had begun reaching out to the Sunni tribes, encouraging them to reject Al Qaeda. With all the factions longing for stability and an end to the fighting, some sort of peace was coming to the Middle East."

"So, just so I understand this correctly. The U.S. invasion of Iraq laid the groundwork for ISIS, I mean Daesh, but the conflicts in Syria allowed them to flourish?"

"Yes and no," Sayed said, "as with everything in the Middle East there is more to it. During the war in Iraq, Al Qaeda would frequently travel back and forth between Syria and Iraq to resupply and regroup, so it had established a long list of contacts in the country. When Assad began killing his own people, turning the peaceful uprising into a civil war, Al Qaeda in Iraq saw its opportunity to grow and establish a presence there. Under Abu Bakr al-Baghdadi, it moved into Syria, merged with its Syrian counterpart and renamed itself as The Islamic State of Iraq and Syria, in short ISIS. This clashed with Al Qaeda's leadership since they had already been establishing a separate branch in Syria, known as Al-Nusra Front. The two groups' turf war added to the already increasingly complicated conflict in Syria. The intra-jihadi battle was waged on the battlefields of Syria, Iraq, and beyond, such as Somalia, and northwest Africa. The total withdrawal of the U.S. forces in December 2011 essentially gave Daesh total freedom in movement. This was utilized to recruit and train fighters and plan for a large scale offensive. In the summer of 2014, the group had its breakout moment. In a swift move, it captured Mosul in Iraq and drove south until it was on the borders of Baghdad. A few weeks later it officially labeled itself as a Caliphate and demanded that all Muslims pledge allegiance. At this point, with bin Laden dead and Al Qaeda dead in the water, groups like Boko Haram in Nigeria and Ansar Beit Al Maqdis in Egypt's Sinai began pledging allegiance and flew the black flag of ISIS. They also established presences in half a dozen other countries."

Sayed sat back in his chair and sipped on his wine. He knew this was a lot of information, but vital to understand the basics of this conflict.

"As you can see, there are many moving parts and even more interests involved. The various groups who changed their pledges of allegiance based on whatever organization is dominating the field are a perfect example of how one agenda is being put on hold to gain strength through allying themselves with someone stronger. I have no doubt in my mind, that most fighters who join Daesh are not the most pious, but rather seek to fulfill whatever goal they have through the current influence of the group."

"This actually leads to the biggest question on my mind. Tell me more about the recruiting of fighters, please. What makes it so appealing to foreigners to join them?" Bastian asked.

"I am not sure that I can give you a satisfying or conclusive answer to that question,' Sayed said. "Like I mentioned, everyone has their own individual motivation. Daesh utilizes an aggressive social media and viral video strategy, using various webpages, Twitter and Facebook accound etc. The only purpose of them is to engage with sympathizers and glorify violence. It started with videos of beheadings, such as the one of U.S. journalist James Foley. It didn't stop there though. There have been filmed executions through drowning, explosives, burning alive, and shootings. Also, when they captured northern Iraqi town of Sinjar, it essentially institutionalized slavery and rape of the Yazidi Christian minority. A reign of barbaric terror to intimidate any opposition and solidify their position. This projected an image of power and independence. Just imagine: you are a confused young man of Middle Eastern descent, somewhat without a guide to point you in the right direction. You don't really fit in with the country you live in, nor with the one your parents came from. Here comes Daesh, offering you purpose, belonging and material rewards, even a bride. All you have to do is to join the movement against the evil empire that is holding sway over the lands. Sounds very Star Wars like, doesn't it?"

"Wow," Bastian said. "I can understand that all this can seem intriguing and fascinating to some, but it's quite ridiculous, or even ironic that Daniel had refused to join the German military and did a civil service instead, officially claiming to consciously be opposing violence," probably because he wanted to do the opposite of what I had done, he thought. "And now he has completely dropped everything to join a military group in some country he's never even been to, and where he knows no one," he continued.

"Yes," the professor agreed. "It's quite the deal for Daesh, wouldn't you say? They don't have enough military in Syria, so with the help of Internet and technology they convince people from other countries to die for their cause with the promise of martyrdom. Utilize the magical tools and promises of Hollywood, to fight the very thing they represent. Generally speaking though from what I have been gathering, there seems to be three types of recruits: the self-proclaimed protector of faith, the one in search of purpose and the tag along. Which one do you think your brother is?"

The party fell quiet for a few minutes while Adnan and Hafsa started cleaning the table. The professor finished his wine while studying Bastian who was staring out into the air with a glazed look and seemed to have become unaware of his environment, until Bastian finally broke the silence.

"No." Bastian concluded. "Daniel is not a martyr. This is not like him. I have to talk to him. If I can just find out where he is and contact him, I can convince him to come back home. And if I can do it quickly, maybe the police won't realize what he's actually been up to, and he won't be arrested when he comes home."

Bastian noticed the doubtful expressions on both Adnan and his father's face, but they were too considerate to say anything.

"I don't mean to discourage you, Sayed said, but it is not that simple. It's not like you will be able to just call him and talk him out of it. And even you could convince him, for what I understand, Daesh does not take kindly to deserters. Instead, may I suggest you go and visit the Fussilet mosque on Friday? I've never been to it myself, but many mosques are open before and after prayers," he explained. "You could stop by and just be honest. Tell them that you're trying to get in touch with your brother, and you know he used to attend this mosque."

"You think they would tell me anything?" Bastian asked doubtfully.

"I don't know," the professor answered. "But it's worth a shot. Until then, you both need to focus on your final exams. I know they're coming up next week, and there's nothing you can do until next Friday anyway Bastian, so try not to think about it."

Adnan saw the look of desperation and helplessness on his friend's face.

"Tell you what," he said, "how about we focus on the exam this week and I will come with you Friday? That way I can make sure to soak up some of your constitutional law knowledge and keep you out of trouble!"

"You would do that for me?" Bastian asked.

"Of course, besides it works in my favor as well."

Adnan smirked and slapped his friend on the back. Sayed didn't like the thought of his son possibly exposing himself to danger from radicals or the authorities, but he knew this was the right thing to do. He looked at them and nodded. The three knew this was an important moment, but that profound feeling quickly disappeared to the sound of Justin Bieber's 'Love Yourself' blaring through the apartment. Sayed and Bastian faintly smiled and rolled their eyes, with Adnan screaming

"HAFSA!" while storming towards her room.

"I will take that as my queue to go home,' Bastian said.

CHAPTER 5

The movement to the target had been flawless and quiet. To avoid any surprises, the helicopter had dropped him and his 5 men team off about 2 km from the compound. The mission was to capture or kill a high value target. From the info they had received, this should be an easy raid. The person of interest was visiting his parents and had brought only a 4 man security team to avoid any suspicions.

Bastian had always preferred to do thing like this at night. The Taliban and their sympathizers didn't have a night vision goggles and didn't fight at night. This gave Bastian's team the advantage and minimized the risk of a firefight or too many casualties. Something especially important to him, since this was his last mission before heading home. Seeing the world through the green colors night vision goggles produce always had something eery to it. Especially when moving in near complete silence.

Despite the cool mountain air, he was sweating heavily. They were moving quickly to, the less time they were on the ground the better. Finally, they reached the compound. Just like in their rehearsals, they stacked up to the side of the main gate while the breaching charges were set. Everyone gave their thumbs up. "3, 2, 1, GO!" The charges went off and blew the gate off its hinges. With this the race was on. 90 seconds to clear the main building and the separate prayer hut.

"Slow is smooth, smooth is fast" Bastian was thinking.

They had been doing this for months now and the entire team moved like a well-oiled machine. They had cleared the prayer hut when the door to the main building opened. Through his night vision Bastian saw a silhouette, a man, holding an AK-47. Pht, pht, pht. The only noise his suppressed rifle made. The body dropped to the ground. "Good shot. And the door is open now.' one of Bastian's teammates said. Bastian moved forward, into the house. He moved down the narrow hallway to the dining table in the living room where his mother was next to the table with the pink flowers in a glass vase. She just stared at him. He turned to the door of the small guest room which had been Daniel's. The door was open. Bastian took a step forward and he was on the beach, overlooking the ocean, dressed in traditional Arab clothes. Not far from him by the water he saw a man facing him, dressed in all black, his face covered, standing over a man in an orange jumpsuit. He pointed a knife in his right hand at Bastian, pulled the head of the man in the jumpsuit back and jammed his blade into the man's neck to behead him.

"What troubles you, brother?" Daniel asked with a smile.

Bastian looked at his brother's face, but before he could answer, Daniel drove the blood covered serrated steel blade of the knife he had just used to cut the man's head off into his brother's chest.

"La 'illah 'illa alllah, brother." Bastian didn't feel pain, but he was falling into darkness. He heard Daniel's voice saying "Alllah 'akbar. Alllah 'akbar...."

Bastian sat up in his bed, panting, drenched in sweat. He was used to periodic nightmares, but this was different. He walked around his apartment to calm himself down. Feeling the cool wood floor under his feet helped him center himself, to calm his breathing. He went to the kitchen to get something to drink. He took a large bottle of water out of the fridge and downed a few large gulps. Then he just stood there in his boxers in the kitchen, pressing the cold bottle against his head.

"What did you do, Daniel?" he thought.

The dream was still vivid in his mind the next day. Although he had tried, Bastian hadn't been able to sleep more that night. The room had felt too hot even after he opened the big window over is bed. After only a few hours, when the morning traffic started, Bastian gave up on sleep. The sound of cars honking and people talking made his dream seem more like what it was - a dream, but he still couldn't shake it. He was now sitting at one of the barstools at his small kitchen table, pouring his second cup of coffee. He always thought the smell was better than the actual taste, but as usual, he drank it anyway for the caffeine.

He checked his Facebook Messenger app on his phone again. Still no answer from Daniel. He hadn't even read it, and it had now been 4 days. Bastian wondered why Daniel hadn't logged on yet. Where was he? What was he doing? Was he safe? Was he even alive? Sayed had been right of course. He tried to shut the thoughts of his brother out. He needed to focus on studying. And he needed to get out of this apartment. Right now it felt too small, almost claustrophobic. After finishing his third cup of coffee, he took a quick, cold shower, got dressed and packed his books. He ran outside just in time to catch the 7:24am bus on his way to the school library.

The next few days went by as though Bastian was in a haze. Every morning he got up early after a nightmare filled night, went to the library to study for his exam and then spent the afternoons practicing Krav Maga at the dojo he had been training at for the last few years. It was a full contact martial arts, originally designed by Imi Lichtenfeld, who used his skills defending the Jewish quarter in Bratislava, Czechoslovakia against fascist groups during the mid to late 1930s. It was a combination of different techniques taken from boxing, wrestling, Judo, Aikido and others. The focus was on real-world situations, efficiency and devastating counter attacks. Bastian's instructor used to be a Krav Maga instructor for the Isreali Defense Force and loved to make the training more challenging for Bastian, knowing he had been in the military as well. Bastian was by no means an outstanding fighter. More often than not he lost his sparring matches. Nevertheless, it was a good change of pace and helped him socialize with likeminded people, some of them sharing similar military experiences as himself. Yet, he eagerly anticipated the end of the week and his visit to the mosque with Adnan.

Bastian and Adnan's consistent studying paid off during the exams, which took place over 3 days for several hours each. Bastian thought this to be one of the strange things about the university. Students studied hours upon hours to do well on the exams. Especially finals always loomed as this big culminating event at the end of the semester. Professors stressed how important it was to do well on them over and over. Once they had finished though, the question was always 'Now what?' To him it always seemed very anticlimactic.

CHAPTER 6

The day after the last final exam. It was a beautiful Wednesday. The sun was shining with the warmth that indicates spring is turning to summer. Bastian and Adnan were sitting outside a small cafe in Kreuzberg. Bergmannstrasse used to be the place to go for anything punk and alternative. Bastian remembered this area from when he was in high school. It was a great place to hang out with friends. Despite the politically motivated graffiti and occupied buildings here there, the area had something energetic, yet peaceful to it. The half a mile street used to be lined with small shops selling punk style clothing, novelties, old books, second hand clothing and whatever else not-mainstream, ant-establishment you can imagine. Even Daniel used to frequent the area before he converted to Islam. Bastian sat with his back against the wall, positioned with his chair so that he could observe the street and its people. Every few moments, his gaze swept along an 180 degree angle. He was well aware where he was and that the level of danger in this street was not even remotely close to what he experienced on his deployments. Yet, this was a habit that comforted him. Aside from keeping him aware of his surroundings, it also provided him with an opportunity to look at the local female population. A fact Adnan thoroughly enjoyed as well. They had their fair share of locker room talk since they met and it was almost as though they were competing on who would spot the best looking women. Despite their talk and gazing Olympics, neither usually tried to spark up a conversation with any of the women they spotted. As it turns out, despite their confident posture in daily life, both were in a way not confident or at least smooth enough to do just that. As focused as they usually were on their studies, the lack of social smooth talking skills did not bother them much. Even less so today, due to the grave situation at hand.

"So, how do you want to approach our little mosque stakeout?" Adnan asked.

"First of all, it's not a stakeout. We have to go in, find the right person to talk to, get the info we need and walk back out"

"Oh, that easy, huh?"

"Yep. So, what is the protocol? What do I do on my first visit?"

"Seriously? Dude, my first prayer at the mosque was when I was 3 and my father was holding my hand when I walked in. I don't know how that would work for a tall, pale guy like you..."

"Shut up, I am serious. What should I do? I mean, I can't just go up to the imam and say I want to learn about Daesh."

"Hmm, you are right, that might be a little too direct. I know my dad is a little better at socializing in those kind of settings. How about him holding your hand?"

"You want me to hold your dad's hand while walking into the mosque? I mean, I saw similar stuff between men in Afghanistan, but I am not sure that would be the right approach here."

"No, stupid. I didn't mean it literally. More figuratively. We could meet with my dad in an hour and he can coach you on the subtleties of not just the praying, but also the talking."

"What do you mean, praying?"

"Really? What did they teach you in the military?"

"Slightly different things that were geared towards our survival and direct conflict with an enemy, which is probably the reason for the problems we had in those countries. We didn't have much time to learn the subtleties of the Islamic culture."

"OK. Thing is, we have to pass you off as a muslim. Not necessarily as an experienced one."

"Right, go on."

"Looking at the guys who came back from fighting in Syria, we can see somewhat of a pattern. A lot of them are newly converts that were, let's say coached, to think it would be a great idea to go to Syria and shoot people. In that sense, you would actually fit in to a certain extent, since you were trained to do just that. We just have to make sure you are a believable Muslim."

"You know, that does sound like a decent idea. Is your dad going to be available today?"

"Oh yes, I already texted him. He is grading papers and said he definitely needs a break. He said to come over in about an hour."

"Perfect! Do you want to leave now?"

"Slow down, buddy. I still want to finish my beer. And enjoy the view a little more," Adnan said with a wink of his eye.
Bastian was relieved to have his friend here with him. He lacked the cultural insight to the Islamic faith and culture, his brother had immersed himself with. This insight was key to find out more about Daniel's whereabouts.

They stayed for another 20 minutes before heading to Adnan's father. It seemed as though Adnan was taking deliberately more time to finish his drink. Most likely due to the tall blonde woman leaving a book store, who Bastian had pointed out to his friend a few minutes earlier. After paying their check, they got into Adnan's car and got on the way.

An hour later they were at the family apartment.

"Welcome back, Bastian," Sayed said. "This will take some time, so I hope you didn't have any plans for the rest of the day"

"Yes, absolutely. I can stay as long as it takes."

"Very well. I will focus for now on the 10 general steps of the prayer. We can take care of the other things later. I also took the liberty to write down the words for the chants in between movements. Think of it all as a dance."

"I am not much of a dancer, but I will do my best." Bastian said.

"Let's begin: Assume a relaxed posture, raise both hands up to the ears with your palms facing the direction of Mecca and say: Allah Akbar - God is great. Your next step is to place your right hand over your left hand on your navel and keep your eyes focused on the place you are standing. Do not let your eyes wander. Then say:
Audhu billahi min ashshayta nirrajeem - "I seek God's shelter from Satan, the condemned"

Bis milla hirrahma nirraheem. Alhamdu lillahi rabbil aalameen. Arrahmaa nirraheem. Maliki yaumiddeen. Iyyaka nabudu wa iyyaka nasta'een. Ihdi nassira talmustaqeem. Sira talladhina
anamta alayhim, ghayril maghdubi alayhim, wa ladhdhaal leen. (Aameen) -
"In the name of God, the most Gracious, most Merciful. All praise is due to God, Lord of the Worlds, The most Gracious, the most Merciful, Master of the Day of Judgment, You alone we worship and You alone we ask for assistance. Guide us along the straight path. The path of those upon whom You have bestowed Your blessings, not the path of those with whom You are angry nor the path of those who have gone astray."

You can read along for now with the cards I gave you, but before going to prayer you definitely should have memorized the words.

"Ok," responded a very focused Bastian.

For the next several hours, Sayed and Adnan went over the details of the prayer with him. They made sure the choreography of the prayer was precise and Bastian knew it by heart. When they finally decided to call it a night with the practice, he had learned the exact body movements and what key words to listen for to bow at the right moments. As they all expected, the words were the more difficult part. Bastian knew he didn't have to be perfect with it, but he needed to be convincing that his conversion had been sincere and that he strived for perfection in his prayer.

After he said his goodbyes to head home, it was close to midnight. Sayed and Adnan stood at the window and watched Bastian disappear into the night. Before going to bed himself, Sayed put his right hand on Adnan's left shoulder and said:

"Just promise me you will be careful."

Adnan didn't turn around, being deep in thought himself and only responded with "I will".

While standing on the platform, waiting for his train home, Bastian stared off into the distance. In his right jacket pocket, his hand clasped the book Sayed had given him. He was not sure why, but he felt conflicted. In a brief moment, while Adnan was in the kitchen, Sayed had approached him with the book he was holding now and with a soft voice had told him

"I know your intentions are good and you are doing this to bring your brother back home safely. Yet, I want you to consider that this is also a matter of religion, of faith. My faith. I urge you to read the words in this book. They are not written in the purity of Arabic, but they still carry the message. Allah is merciful and I want you to have mercy in your heart as well. I know you are angry with Daniel and cannot understand his actions. People will do things we don't understand, but it is on us, on you to practice forgiveness. This will help you not only to be convincing at the mosque, but also in life beyond your quest. Inshallah - God willing."

Bastian had had briefings and courses on radical Islam and some of the general Islamic teachings before, but it never affected him as much as what Sayed had told him. It wasn't the words, rather how he had said them. There was something in his eyes when he spoke of Islam, true conviction. It wasn't hate that Bastian saw, it was love and compassion. Things he had never connected with Islam. He didn't make a conscious decision when he took out the book and started to read while standing on that platform. It simply happened and felt right. Reading always relaxed him, but not like this. This gave him encouragement, it was calming. He wouldn't stop reading until well into the night after he arrived at his apartment.

CHAPTER 7

He was surrounded by the rubble of destroyed buildings. They had been driving for what must have been days. He knew it had been 2 sunrises since the capture. To avoid detection by coalition aircraft, they had been consistently moving, changing locations and vehicles every few hours. He had been sitting here for a while now. Unsure what was going on, he wasn't even sure he cared. Smell of diesel fuel was in the air.

One of the men had given him something weird tasting earlier. Ever since then his level of caring for anything had dropped consistently. He knew from his mission briefings that Daesh preferred to drug its captives to be able to control them easier, with their substance of choice being opium. The onset was relatively quick, maybe about five minutes. There was an incredible sense of relaxation, so intense that he had lost the will to move his body. He was sitting on the floor, legs crossed, his head just hanging down. For what felt like an eternity he had been staring at the legs of the jumpsuit he had been given. The color seemed intense, bright. He could feel his legs tingling from sitting for too long in this position, but he didn't want to get up. He noticed some movement from the corner of his eyes. Several men appeared, working busily around him. He wanted to look at what was going on, but he didn't. It wasn't impossible for him to move, but it just took more effort than he felt he had. His head was swimming with random thoughts and he could not comprehend what was happening around him. So many lights, some men arguing over a canister of some sorts, while others set up cameras at different angles. He was tired; his body was tired. Somehow, it actually felt pleasant.

The scene before him seemed to become more ordered. Things did suddenly quiet down when a man dressed in jeans and a t-shirt walked up. He told one of them next to a camera to get ready to record. Was he speaking English? He noticed the red recording lights on the cameras. All of them pointed at him.

Suddenly the fog in his mind lifted. He sensed something was going to happen. Adrenaline started to flood his mind, but the opium wouldn't let him move. The smell of the diesel fuel that had been poured around him was immensely strong. He realized his orange jumpsuit was soaked in diesel as well. He recognized this part from his briefings as well. This was bad, very bad. They would burn him alive. Most males under a certain age are convinced that given the right set of extreme circumstances, they'd turn into an unstoppable mix of Jet Li and the Hulk. It cannot get much more extreme than realizing the threat to be burnt alive, yet, he could hardly move a limb. He knew the drugs were only partly to blame. He was in a cage, how would he even break free from it, let alone escape the armed men standing not too far around him?

With no other options, he just accepted his fate. He was immobilized, but not in a physical way. There was nothing that held him down, no ties or cuffs that kept him sitting. He was paralyzed by the psychosomatic petrification, the awareness of his acute level of hopelessness. An inner feeling of powerlessness whispered to him that he was past saving. All he could do was maintain his dignity. The man in jeans looked at him intently, almost studying him. When they made eye contact, a smirk on the man's face and something in his eyes changed. They held their gaze while he lit his Zippo lighter and dropped it to a fuel trail by his feet, which extended all the way to the cage that the Jordanian pilot was sitting in.

Whoosh!

The sensation engulfing him was sudden. He had felt the heat of his jet's engines before, but this was entirely different. The fuel on his jumpsuit combined with the air pockets between his skin and the fabric caused the fire to burn hotter and faster than if he had been naked. It is believed that victims of a burning die from smoke inhalation before encountering the worst of the flames. Unfortunately for Abdullah al-Karboly, that was merciful thinking, rather than reality. He tried to move, maybe roll on the ground to extinguish the flames, to save whatever was left of him. The adrenaline his body was pouring out could not overpower the effects of the opium. He felt the searing pain on his legs, his groin, his chest, his face. Flames consumed his lungs when he tried to breathe. His vision became blurred when the liquid in his eyes started to boil and burst his eye balls. Everything turned black. He could feel his body tumbling over. There was no escape, he knew it was almost over. He tried to let out a scream from the pain, but the flames had all but destroyed his chest and head. His vocal chords were already charred and useless. What was left of his mouth stayed open, the flames finding whatever tissue was left. A feeling of peace overcame him. He saw flashes of his parents, his wife, his two young daughters, then nothing.

It all had taken no more than 30 seconds. The man in jeans nodded slightly, already making mental notes on how to edit the footage from the three cameras. "That was intense!", one of the men behind the camera said. "Don't be such a baby", the man in jeans said with a southern drawl. "Make sure ya'll pack everything up and be ready to go in 10. I'll have our hosts take us to the extraction point."

CHAPTER 8

It was Friday morning. Bastian was in his bed. He had spent the last 2 days practicing the proper movements for the prayer, as well as pronouncing the words correctly. In the times between practice he had continued to read the Quran Sayed had given him on Wednesday before he left their apartment. Albeit he wasn't very spiritual, he recognized a beauty in the way it was written and the message it provided. Being the skeptic that he was, he blamed his success in practicing the prayer simply on his liking of the text.

As always, he had woken up early, around 5 am. Adnan would not be picking him up for another few hours. While he usually got up to exercise or read, he decided to just be lazy today and stay in bed. He spent the next hour or so letting his mind wander, just staring at the ceiling.

Adnan arrived at Bastian's place at 11:30 am. When Bastian opened the door for his friend, Adnan's first words were:

"Parking really sucks in this area, man. You should move to a better place."

"Guess why I don't have a car," Bastian responded.

"So? You should be more considerate of the parking needs of your guests," Adnan jokingly replied.

They had decided to use public transportation to get to the mosque, figuring it would be faster, but also not to give anyone the opportunity to follow them later using Adnan's license plate. It seemed a little over the top and paranoid at first to Adnan, but his friend insisted.

They had arrived just before lunchtime prayers. The Fussilet mosque was located in a residential area of Moabit, Berlin. It was in an older apartment building. You would never know it was a mosque if you passed by the building. For obvious reasons, there were no minarets or other markings on the outside indicating a house of worship as Bastian had expected. All it had was one sign by the main door, which read

„Hicret-Camii - Fussilet 33 e.V." Typical for Germany, this was not an official mosque, but a registered religious group. This allowed for an easier process in founding and maintaining a religious community. Bastian had noticed, they were only 150 feet away from a Shiite group called „Al Hassanein" and directly across from the „Weisheits- und Kulturzentrums", an Indonesian Muslim community.

"If these bastards can get along just fine here, what's stopping them from doing it in their own country?" Bastian thought to himself.

One thing made him smile: Most of the worshippers he saw were dressed in traditional man dress and beard, but most wore some sort of sneakers. Bastian mumbled to Adnan:

"They look like Bin Laden, just with white Jackets and Nike Air Max."

Adnan gave a chuckle, but kept a stern face otherwise. He was looking around to engage people in small talk before prayer. There were 3 people outside talking: 2 young people about college age and an older man, probably in his 60s. The young men seemed to be deep in conversation, while the old man was making his way into the mosque. Adnan and Bastian followed him inside. They stepped inside what served as the foyers. It was covered by lush carpeting, colored in green with gold ornaments. The only things inside the room were a few shelves along the right hand wall. Bastian noted a smell that must have been the mix of dust and the odor of numerous men who had been coming here for a while. It wasn't like a locker room, but still noticeable.

They removed their shoes and placed them on the nearby shelf, before following the old man into the cleansing room, which was off to the left of the foyer. When Sayed had explained to Bastian the procedures of the cleansing, Bastian had envisioned something fancy. Maybe along the lines of a bath house with heavily decorated tiles and mosaics. Even though this was all just a show for him to find out as much as he could about how to find Daniel, he was disappointed. This was only a small and narrow old fashioned apartment bathroom, where the toilet and the bathtub had been removed. Instead there were 5 simple sinks hung relatively low on the wall. Shaking off his misplaced feelings of being let down in his expectations, he went through the ritual of the three washings of hands, wrists, forearms, elbows, faces, hairlines, feet and ankles. Each body section was washed in sequence and had an associated prayer to be uttered. He hadn't been able to memorize all of the words, so instead he mumbled a few phrases. Since this was a very personal ritual, nobody noticed.

The cleansing room had a second doorway leaving to the musallah, the prayer room. Upon entering, Bastian went through the subtle motions of a prayer. He hadn't bothered to memorize the exact prayer and quietly mumbled so as to pretend he was doing it.

"And you should always do two rakat, two little sets of prayer upon entering a mosque," Sayed had explained.

Most of the worshippers were focused on their own rituals and no one seemed to have noticed Bastian faking his way through.

Once done with his fake prayer, he took in the room. He noticed an essential element of a mosque's architecture, the mihrab. It constitutes a niche in the wall that indicates the direction of Mecca, towards which all Muslims pray. The direction of Mecca is called the qibla, and so the wall in which the mihrab is set is called the qibla wall.

In this case, there was only an oversized poster of a very richly decorated mosque, Bastian didn't recognize. As if Adnan had read his mind, "Looks like someone went to the Haga Sophia in Istanbul and brought the poster back as a souvenir." Bastian nodded while taking in the rest of the room. The floor was covered with different kinds of carpets. The wall on the far left featured shelves lined with books, most likely on Islamic philosophy, theology and law, along with collections of the sayings and traditions of Muhammad. At least according to descriptions of mosques Bastian had looked up on the internet. Aside from that and a few other ornamented posters the walls were empty. The lighting in the room was provided by several modern LED light installations, close to the high ceilings.

"Almost like the display section for the home lighting at the local hardware store,' Bastian thought.

Adnan led Bastian around the men already settled in their spots for the prayer. He opted for them to sit in the middle of the room, but off to the side, across from the book shelves, close by the door to the cleansing room. This put them between the mihrab and the placing in the back of the room dedicated for zakat, or charity, where Muslims may donate money to help the poor or to support the mosque. While they waited for the imam, they were accompanied by the familiar sights of the last few people hurrying in, followed by a few latecomers. Bastian noticed one young worshipper, late teens, discreetly checking that he had turned off his cell phone. The imam entered the room and began the service with an opening prayer.

Throughout, men slowly came in and prayed before sitting in any open spot that was available. By the end of the service at 2:30, the room was filled with about 75 men and some boys. Most of the men were Arabic, Middle-Eastern, but Bastian also noticed some Caucasians. After the prayer, a message was given in German for about 30 minutes about Muslim eschatology, concerning death, judgment, and the final destiny of the soul and of humankind.

The references to the Qur'an were given in Arabic first, followed by a German interpretation. The message was delivered in two parts. First was an emphasis on the necessity of trusting and serving God ALONE. Nothing happened without God's permission; and nothing and no one else is worthy of worship, service, and dependence. Second, he spoke about what true "Jihad" is. The 'greater Jihad' was a personal struggle against our own lower nature; the struggle to subdue our own selfish desires in submission to the will of God. This Jihad was aimed at decadence and unbelieving in the truth. Indiscriminate killing of noncombatants, and especially good Muslim women and children, was simply not permitted in Islam. Therefore, a true fighter for jihad only went after unbelievers and sinners. This includes the Shia, who refused to accept the true Islam. Their views were a flagrant violation of the most basic principles of Islam. It was condemned by all who follow God and his Prophet.

After the message, all the men prayed and bowed in unison for several minutes. During the entire service, the mood was somber and respectful. The service closed with some announcements. Most of the men left right after. Very few stayed long afterward to talk with others.

The remainder of the congregation, which was not very large, was very friendly. Adnan and Bastian were introduced to most of them. While Bastian struggled to remember most of those 'strange sounding' names, he remembered a 'Hasan' and an 'Amir'. There was a 'Mike', who, even though he was originally from Iraq, had taken a Western name.
"I stand out like a sore thumb", Bastian thought. He had a point. Most everyone else was dark skinned, in various shadings. Despite this disparity in skin pigmentation, though, there did not appear to be any discomfort on anyone's part.

Adnan excused himself to use the restroom. Bastian, now by himself, tried to mingle with the other people in the room and strike up a conversation. Since everyone seemed to be deep in personal discussions, he used the time to look at the different posters containing designs foreign to him, which lined the walls. Their rhythm was only broken by the periodic posting of flyers taped on top of them that made mention of religious group meetings, events, and the center's impacts on the local community.

"So, what brings you here today?" a man who introduced himself as Othman asked Bastian in a gentle tone.

"To be frank, I don't think the mosque I have been going is true to the word of the prophet."

"What do you mean?"

"When I converted to Islam last year, it was fine. But, the more I learned, the more I felt my Imam and the congregation was frivolous. Men not growing their beards, women coming to prayer without their heads covered. I started listening to Deso Dogg and really liked his lyrics on Kafirs. My friend Ali also showed me some teachings online."

"Your friend Ali?"

"Yes, he is the one who introduced me to Islam in the first place. There he is." Bastian gestured towards Adnan coming back from the restroom.

"So, you are the man who showed our friend the light?!" Othman said more matter of factly.

"Well, I can't really take all the credit," Adnan said, "I was reading texts by Hassan Dabbagh and Thomas here," Adnan pointing at Bastian, "he wanted to know what it was about. So I told him and showed him Abou-Nagie's website "The true religion". From there it didn't take long that he understood and decided to convert."

"You truly are doing Allah's work," Othman said. "Tell me, would you two be interested to join our study group today? It is going to start in a few minutes. We are going to watch a video by Pierre Vogel and afterwards discuss its ideas. There will be food of course."

Pierre Vogel was considered one of the most influential Islamists in Germany. The convert had been an active Islamist preacher since 2006. He was spreading his highly controversial ideas mainly among a young audience; for example, via Internet videos on various web pages. He believed that wearing a full veil was a compulsory duty for all Muslim women. While he said he didn't believe that Islam condoned any physical violence against innocents, terror attacks and honor killings, his definition of innocents was extremely narrow. His interpretation of the scripture pooled the majority of society into the realm of legitimate targets for jihad. His worldview was based on a strict division of Islam, considered as right and good, versus un-Islamic, thus wrong and evil behavior. His sermons had been classified as contributing to the radicalization of individual, very religious youth, and he had been under surveillance by the German security services for some time now.

"Yes, we would like that." Bastian said.

"Very well. I still have to prepare a few things, so just stay around and we will begin soon. Excuse me for a moment."

With that Othman left. Adnan and Bastian stayed in the room and continued mingling with the few remaining visitors. Bastian assumed most of them would be joining them for the study group as well. The talks were mostly casual, pertaining to local soccer clubs and good food places in the area.

After a few minutes someone Bastian didn't recognize wheeled in a TV set connected to a laptop and started to set it up in the middle of the room. Two others brought in several trays of delicious smelling food and bottled water. They seemed to be going through a routine often practiced and finished their task within a few moments. Othman came to join the group and gestured them to gather around the TV. It seemed very relaxed to Bastian, almost like movie day in high school during the "cool teacher's" class session.

"We'll continue today with Pierre Vogel's discussion series titled "Was Jesus a Muslim or Christian." As always, I am encouraging you to visit his website discoveringislam.org and rewatch his lectures. Afterwards we will discuss a little. Feel free to grab some food before we begin. Also, welcome Ali and Thomas to our little group. I hope you enjoy your stay with us and will come regularly."

Adnan and Bastian smiled and tanked Othman for the warm welcome.

Everyone went to get some food and water and then sat in a semi circle around the TV set. Satisfied that everyone was ready, Othman started a video stream from a webpage. On the TV appeared a caucasian male with typical thick German features, sporting traditional islamic clothing and a fire red beard. His demeanor was collected and calm, yet, he did make a knowledgable and almost authoritative impression. Bastian understood why that person was selected to make those videos.

After about 30 minutes of video watching, Othman began to lead the discussion on things that Vogel had addressed, Islam and other related topics that had been brought up. The group spent the next hour and a half talking about the core of the Islamic faith, the role of modern Islam, and the perversions of the faith by secular Muslims straying from the teachings.

Othman's openness to discuss and address such topics was apparent as he spoke, with reason as the anchor of each of his explanations. The conversation shifted to modern historical events and the role of politics in manipulating the tenets of the faith for the personal gains, as well as the aspirations of corrupt and greedy individuals. Othman often cited and summarized passages from the Quran that condemned such immoral behavior outright and tied back to the concepts of faith that had been discussed earlier.

"Now, I want you to understand, we are not perfect, but it is our intent that matters," Othman said.

While most of the teachings from the video and the ones delivered by Othman seemed strange and possibly revolting to Bastian, some things resonated with him. They made sense in combination with the people around him and the general atmosphere of the group. When he had arrived at the mosque, he had judged every single one of them as rag heads and lunatics. Now, sitting amongst them, accepted into this group, Bastian's earlier opinions on them faded. They were just normal people to him.

Othman had shifted the topic to khuruj fi sabilillah, which means going about in the path of God. He stressed that khuruj fi sabilillah is jihad. This is what it means for them. That this should be at the core of every good Muslim's worldview.

Throughout his life and military career, Bastian had always believed that there must be a just cause for violence. Before he left the Bunderswehr, he had developed doubts regarding some of the things he had done overseas and whether some orders were just after all.

"Jihad," Othman explained, "provides a sense of power, in a world where Muslims feel that they are powerless. It gives us pride, in a world where Muslims feel humiliation. Jihad, it also means just violence, because it is violence in the name of Allah. He is the one who allows us to be violent against the unbelievers, he legitimizes to act violently."

The room was quiet and everyone listened intently.

"Various governments, including here in Germany, are trying to stop jihad. They say it is immoral. But who are they? What do they know? How dare they judge us for protecting our faith? In 1996, there was the Russian invasion of Chechnya, so the Chechnya War was our call to Jihad. In 1998, there was Bin Laden's fatwa to kill Americans and Jews, because of American support for Israel and the stationing of troops in the Arabian Peninsula brought on by the betrayal of Kuwait."

The concrete examples from recent history initiated questions by some in the group and they started discussing. The argument started to form and the enemy became everyone not supporting Jihad.

"Look at most of the women here, walking around like prostitutes', Mike said.

Everyone nodded in agreement.

"This is true," Othman said, "and it is on us to change this. To spread the true Islam through Jihad. It starts here, with us, in our neighborhoods."

One of the guys, Mohammed, asked about the Caliphate.

"Ah, yes," Othman replied, "it is a new world and a blessing to have brave Muslims stand up and declare it. The Caliphate, Inshallah, will grow and prosper and eventually encompass the whole world. Let the West come. Let the Americans shoot their rockets, or the regimes in Syria or Iraq try to fight us. We will prevail."

"Have you heard any news from the front?" Mohammed asked.

"Not recently, but I am waiting on word any day." Othman looked at their faces. "I know most of you will ask how you can help the cause. While it is the duty for every good Muslim to fight jihad, not everyone can go and do their part in battle. But there are other means to support our holy soldiers in the fight. Donations, outreach, provide food and shelter for traveling fighters. You should all pray for them. For the ones already there and for the ones making the journey to the Caliphate. Crossing to the Caliphate close to the small Turkish village of Gwer is perilous, but Allah will protect them all."

This was what Bastian had been waiting for. Finally some sort of information.

The meeting ended after 3 hours. They all said their good byes and left. Adnan and Bastian headed to the train station, they had arrived at. Neither noticed the figure in the 3rd floor window across the street from the mosque, taking pictures of them when they left the building. After they had made sure no one had followed them, they exited the train and walked for about 3 miles back to Bastian's place.

After a few minutes into their walk, Adnan ask Bastian what he was thinking.

"This was an interview to join them, but who knows how long it takes. I don't have time for that. Daniel does not have time for that."

"I have a feeling where you are going with this."

"You heard what they said, the village of Gwer. That is where I have to go."

"Are you crazy?"

"What other option do I have? Don't you read the news? The conflict had been intensifying. More ground troops are being deployed. More air strikes.... No, I have to find him and bring him back. You saw the guys in that meeting. Most of them don't speak Arabic. Daesh must have brigades just for them. Or interpreters or something. I think, if I can get into Turkey and then get to that village, there is a good chance for me to find him."

"You mean for us to find him!?"

While Bastian knew he needed help, he declined Adnan's offer.

"I can't ask you to come with me."

"You don't have to ask."

"Your father will never let you."

"I will tell only the basics. Maybe that I am only taking you to the border to make sure you don't do anything stupid on the way."

"I don't know..."

Hey, I am not giving you an option here, Bastian. I am coming with you and that is it. You are family, like a lost brother. One that balances out Hafsa's horrible taste in music."

"OK, then let's meet tomorrow at my place and plan it out. I want to leave as soon as possible."

"OK"

CHAPTER 9

Early morning the next day. Bastian hadn't gotten much sleep that night. After coming home he had immediately started his preparations. Using Google maps, weather reports and various other resources, he had to decide what gear to take based on the weather and terrain he would encounter. He had decided to pack light and only use a small backpack he had gotten as a gift from an American unit he worked with while serving in Afghanistan. He liked this specific piece of gear especially for traveling. It was black and very inconspicuous while the same time offering a lot of space to pack different type of things you would need on this trip. Additionally it would serve the purpose to give the impression that he was there to stay, that the Islamic state would be his permanent home. The disadvantage in taking only a small backpack on a plane was that he wasn't able to take any kind of tactical gear with them such as a knife or any other weapon. He decided to purchase a good knife when he got to Turkey, before he made his driving towards the border. The things he packed were simple but sturdy and served the purpose. He packed three pairs of underwear, three pairs of good boots socks, three pairs of T-shirts, all dark and single colored, as well as one pair of spare pants, made from the same material as the ones he would be wearing on the flight and his trip for the most part. The material was the same material used for fire hoses, a type of very heavy cotton, extremely sturdy, but looking like a regular pair of pants. He chose a pair of well broken in Danner boots. Before they had parted ways, he had instructed Adnan to pack similar attire to make sure his friend was properly clothed for the trip ahead. After he was done packing he just laid on his bed, staring at the ceiling not quite sure what he should be doing next.

He closed his eyes and let his thoughts wander. When he opened his eyes, it was dark outside. He must have fallen asleep. Slightly disoriented, he sat up on his bed and looked around the dark apartment. He thought there was a noise that had woken him up. He tried to focus and listened for it again. Something was not right. There it was again. It sounded like someone shuffling around in front of his apartment door. Before Bastian could move, the door was broken down and several men stormed into his small living space, yelling for him to get on the floor, pointing guns at him. Knowing he didn't have a chance to escape he complied and laid face down on the floor. One of the masked men put his knee onto Bastian's neck to prevent him from moving, while another man tied his hands with zip ties behind his back. Once his hands were secured, they sat him up on his knees. As quickly as the chaos had ensued, everything fell silent again. Bastian tried to look around, get a better feel for his attackers. The moment he turned his head though, one of the masked men standing behind Bastian smacked him in the back of his head hard.

"Eyes to the ground," he growled.

He complied, figuring it would be easier to go along with it for now.

Another man closer to the apartment door gestured to someone outside and said:

"We are good, you can come in now."

In stepped a man Bastian knew from the execution videos he had watched to find out more about what he was dealing with. Mohammed Emwazi, whom the press referred to as Jihadi John. Emwazi had been been part of a four-person terrorist cell from England. Because of their English accents, some freed hostages had referred to them as The Beatles. He had gained some notoriety through his dramatic pre-execution speeches, aimed at world leaders.
His posture was that of a man in control. With a smug look on his face he told Bastian:

"Look at me! Oh slave of your government, oh mule of the Jews. How strange it is that we find ourselves today, that an insignificant infidel like you challenges the might of the Islamic State. One would have thought you would have learned the lessons of your pathetic master in Washington and his failed campaign against Islamic State. It seems that you are just as arrogant and foolish. In fact Sebastian, you are more of an imbecile. Only an imbecile would dare to wage war against a land where the law of Allah reigns supreme. And where the people live under the justice and security of the Sharia.

Only an imbecile would dare to anger a people who love death the way that you love your life.

Do you really think your Government cares about now? Or will they abandon you, as they have abandoned the spies, and those who came before them? Because you will lose this war, as you lost in Iraq and Afghanistan."

Bastian was trying to say something. Anything to wipe that smug look off Emwazi's face. Yet, he could not utter a single word.

"Let me show you what happens to anyone who challenges us."

With that, Emwazi flashed the knife he had used in all of his videos. He stepped forward and squatted down in front of Bastian. They were now on eye level, gazing at each other. Bastian thought of how easy it would be to head butt this savage now. Break his nose and teach him a lesson. He could use the ensuing chaos to tackle the man by the door and make his escape. They must have predicted his thoughts. The two men behind him pushed down on his shoulders, making it impossible for him to move.
Emwazi brought up the knife to Bastian's throat.

"I am sure you have seen some of our videos and are expecting me to cut your head off. That would be too easy for you though, too quick. I need you to learn from this. Don't worry, once you bled out, I will still cut your head off. And send it as a gift to your mother."

Before he had finished saying the word "mother" he plunged the knife into Bastian's neck, whose eyes opened wide. Heart pounding in his ears, he closed his eyes and tried to scream. When he looked, the Emwazi and his men had disappeared. Breathing heavy, sweating and with a racing heart Bastian looked left, out of the window of the Turkish Airlines flight TK4 bound for Ankara. Adnan was sound asleep in the seat to his right.

"That was intense," Bastian told himself while trying to get his breathing under control

CHAPTER 10

This was Daniel's day, something he had been anxiously waiting for the last 2 weeks. Out of security concerns, they had been zig zagging through rugged terrain for more than 3 hours.

"We'll be there in 5 minutes," the driver called out in Arabic.

What no one in Daniel's company was aware of, nearly three miles above them, American eyes silently tracked the SUVs and the pickup truck that made up Daniel's little convoy. Within a few hundred meters from Daniel's destination, a dozen U.S. special operations soldiers, known as an A-Team, were positioned in a hilltop. They had been dropped off by helicopter five miles south of the compound hours earlier with the mission to capture or kill high value members of the Islamic State. The team was led by an Army captain, a veteran of multiple tours in Afghanistan. Under U.S. military rules, the captain, as the ground force commander, was responsible for deciding whether to order an airstrike.

The convoy reached the compound and everyone got out of the vehicles. Daniel, along with the men he had been living and fighting with since he arrived in Syria, were welcomed with drums and huge cheers in the main building meant for the ceremony. All the guests made an effort to congratulate him warmly one by one and giving him nothing but the best wishes that him and his soon to be bride would have a happy and fruitful life together in the service to Allah. Daniel had never met his bride before. It was all arranged through one of his superiors, Abu Abbad. All he knew was, the she had been a convert from the Netherlands, who had decided to join the Islamic State and had arrived 2 week prior to the ceremony.

The compound and its main building were decorated with Islamic State flags and the majority of the guests were fighters with their multiple wives. Numerous kids were running around.

"We have 18 pax dismounted and moving towards the main building at this time," an Air Force pilot said from a cramped control room at Wallace Air Force Base in Nevada, more than 6,000 miles away.

He was the sensor operator of the unmanned vehicle observing the building from above. Another pilot was flying the Predator drone remotely, using the joystick in his right hand. The live video transmissions from the Syrian sky was complemented by the radio of the unit on the ground. The Predator was a propeller-driven drone, with a medium-altitude and missile carrying capabilities. It was equipped with several cameras, including infrared devices that allowed it to continue flight and surveillance at night. Contrary to its heavily armed version, the MQ-9 Reaper, the Predator could carry only two Hellfire missiles. Fully fueled, the 27-foot- long craft remotely controlled aircraft could remain aloft for as long as 24 hours.

"Roger, Joker Actual's intent is to destroy the vehicles and the personnel," came the A-team commander's reply, using his call sign.

"Joker Actual this is Slasher 3, solid copy. Break, break. Be advised, on the east side of the compound there are additional vehicles. About 50 pax total present, including various children. Majority of the dismounts are moving into structure located to the north of the gate. See if you can get eyes on that compound. Compound has multiple movers as well as one pickup truck hot."

"Slasher 3, this Joker Actual. Affirm, WILCO", the Special Forces commander replied. He signaled his men to move in closer to get a better view of the activities.

The ceremony commenced inside the main building of the compound, which normally served as the community hall for the village. Daniel met his bride for the first time at the entrance to the building. She was wearing a richly decorated white wedding gown, with a full veil covering her head and face. Several full veiled women ushered around her to ensure her graceful and decent appearance throughout the wedding. One of them lifted his bride's veil so they could see each other.
Daniel smiled at her and said:

" 'Ant jamilat kama qal li 'abu eabad. - You are as beautiful as Abu Abbad told me."

Her face was stoic, no sign of emotion. She closed her eyes and gave him the hint of a nod. Her eyes seemed dull, almost lifeless.

"Take my arm" Daniel said as he extended his left elbow.

She linked her right arm with his and both started walking inside the building. At an even pace they moved towards the couches they were going to sit on during the ceremony. She was walking slower than Daniel and more deliberate in her steps. He wondered for a brief moment, but assumed it was because of the dress. He didn't know that she had been raped for over three days by Abu Abbad and his two most trusted guards, who were all in attendance. Her ordeal had ended only hours before they had dropped her at the compound this morning for the wedding. Abu Abbad had been Daniel's mentor ever since he had arrived in Syria. Being a high level member of the Islamic State leadership and responsible for Al-Hayat, he had volunteered to select a wife for Daniel and pay for the wedding.

The imam began the ceremony with the recitation of the Holy Quran, and hymns praising the prophet. Then, after the sermon was recited with the terms and conditions of the matrimonial contract, Daniel and his new bride uttered their acceptance of them by saying "*qubool* " "yes" three times, making the marriage valid. This concluded the nikah and the walimah could begin.

Customarily, after Muslims marry, they must make a public announcement of the marriage. This announcement celebration, was called the walimah. With Daniel seated on the couch and his newlywed wife sitting to his left, the guests congratulated them and gave them gifts and money.

"Slasher3 to Joker Actual." The Air Force pilot controlling the drone radioed to the men on the ground.

"Send it for Joker Actual" came the reply.

"The compound with the rendezvous, there's an additional pickup truck, appears hot as well and we're tracking multiple personnel throughout. How copy?"

"Solid copy." The commander replied. He then whispered to his sniper "Keep an eye on the guys by the truck."

"Roger" the man behind the rifle grunted.

Looking through the thermal scope of his Remington 700 bolt action rifle, chambered in .300 Win Mag, he could clearly make out the heat signatures of several guards, as well as the heat coming off the truck in question. Tracking people at night like that always reminded him of the Schwarzenegger movie "Predator". He let out a snarl, mimicking the sound the beast made in the movie.

The celebration was in full swing. Daniel thought for a moment how much more lively the festivities would be with alcohol. The Islamic State was strict on not allowing the consumption of alcohol. While he knew it was better this way, he did have moments were he missed his party days. He shook off that thought and instead indulged in the large amounts of food. The Quran described the Prophet Muhammad slaughtering a goat and providing bread for one of his walimahs. Accordingly, the food today consisted of different types of meat, such as goat, lamb and chicken. Also dates, hummus, tabbouleh, fattoush, labneh, mujaddara, shanklish, bastirma, sujuk, baklava, dried yogurt and butter. In short, it was a feast and everyone enjoyed it. Their struggle against the infidels had taken a toll and food was not always this plentiful. This was a special occasion though, which warranted to splurge. Some of the women had also brought candies and sweet desserts, which were enjoyed by the kids that were milling around the other guests. Daniel wasn't sure how many there were, but it must have been close to 30.

"Joker Actual to Slasher 3"

"Send it for Slasher 3."

"Just giving you a heads up we're increasing…." There was a moment of radio static. "….maneuvering on all four sides *garbled radio* so any kind of movement you see, possible link ups or any signs of this starting to disperse just give me a heads up. How copy?"

"Solid copy."

The soldiers on the ground silently moved to set up in an L-shape. This tactic got its effects from an intensifying concentration of fire by overlapping the individual fields of fire. When he settled in to his new overwatch position, the sniper whispered over the team's radio:

"In position. Got a sweet view on the target."

"They're going to do something nefarious," one of the other soldiers chimed in over the team's radio.

"Salla alllah ealayh wasallam mae burakatih waladayk hayatan hayila - May Allah bless you both with His blessings and you have a tremendous life" Abu Abbad said to Daniel, while presenting him with elaborately decorated eggs as a symbol of fertility.

He was flanked by his two grim looking bodyguards.
"Shukraan, Abu Abbad" Daniel said.

He wondered if his bodyguards ever left his side. Or whether they were able to smile. After all these months in Syria, he had yet to see it.

"Are you already leaving?"

"Yes, I must apologize. I have to hurry back to Raqqa for meetings on how to deal with the encroaching Iraqi forces. They have been gaining ground around Mosul."

"Inshallah - God willing, we will defeat them soon." Daniel said.

"Yes, yes, we will. Don't let this bother you for now. This is your night. Enjoy it." Abu Abbad said.

He had been like a father to Daniel ever since had arrived. He had even insisted on paying for the wedding. Daniel's admiration and gratitude for the man who had welcomed him into the Islamic State with open arms ran deep. He wished he could have stayed and celebrated with him. He knew though that the defense of Mosul from the Iraqi army was important. He watched Abu Abbad and his protectors exiting the building quickly to get to their vehicles.

"OK, something is happening now. Joker Actual be advised, we have 3 pax exiting the building and 4 more converging on two trucks closest to the gate. How copy?"

"Joker Actual copies"

"Wouldn't surprise me if this was one of their important guys, you know what I mean?" The pilot said to the sensor operator sitting to his right.

"Yeah, he's got his security detail." The sensor operator replied.

"Joker Actual be advised, two trucks with 7 pax leaving the compound at high speed. Not sure whether the meeting is over. How do you want to proceed?" The pilot radioed the commander on the ground."

"Slasher 3, this is Joker Actual. Give us 2 more minutes to get in position. Requesting weapons hot."

Being somewhat depressed his mentor had left so early, Daniel walked outside the building to get some fresh air and to relive himself. Some of the fighters were outside. When they saw Daniel they starting chanting and firing their weapons into the air in celebration.

"Joker Actual this is Slasher 3. Ok we're all set up, up here; standby your intentions for fire mission. Be advised, we see gun fire from the compound. How copy?"

"No shit, I can see and hear that myself" the A-team commander mumbled. "Roger, ground force commander's intent is to destroy the vehicles and the personnel."

"Roger, stand by for engagement." the pilot responded. He nodded to the sensor operator next to him and said "Understand we are clear to engage.

"Stand by. 3, 2, 1…." the sensor operator counted down, "missile is a go, 5 seconds to impact."

"Roger … and there it goes!" The pilot said to himself.

The missile had been released from the clamps that held it in place under the wing of the Predator and was now racing towards its target. 5 seconds. Daniel heard a faint noise and wasn't sure what to make of it. 4 seconds. He turned around to face the fighters 20 meters away from him, still shooting their rifles in the air, laughing and shouting at him. 3 seconds. He heard the music from inside the building, nearly drowned out by the sound of the AK 47 rifles being shot. 2 seconds. He smiled, thinking how lucky he was to have such a lovely bride and a bright future in the Islamic State. 1 second. Daniel thought about how much he missed his mother and Bastian. Impact.

There was a bright flash, followed by a massive explosion. He felt being thrown backwards by a massive force, slamming him hard into the compound wall. Everything went dark.

"Slasher 3 to Joker Actual, we have a good hit. Target destroyed. How copy?"
"Solid copy. Standing by to clear stragglers before extract."

"Roger. Slasher 3 going off station."

"Do you see anything moving through the thermals?" The commander asked his sniper over the team radio.

"Negative, they are done" came the reply.

"Alright, pack up, boys. Let's make our way to the extract point."

With no enemy forces in sight after the explosion, the soldiers quickly got up and began their hike back south to meet up with the helicopters that would take them back to base.

END PART 1

Made in the USA
Las Vegas, NV
07 February 2022

43345428R00038